OUT THERE

VOLUME 1

B. A. PAUL

CONTENTS

FOREWORD

Small children love asking "Why?" Some preschoolers I've interacted with can concoct a string of Whys starting at sunup that can circle the earth twice before the yellow orb flops below the western horizon in exhaustion.

When *my* kids were small they were worry warts. They didn't much care about the why of a thing. They wanted to know all possible outcomes and have a plan for every potential negative event.

What if this, what if that?

And oh-so-many Yeah-Buts when they weren't happy with the answers to the What-Ifs. It's a hazard of living with a control-freak mommy who, likewise, liked to plan out to the Nth degree every bit of the day.

And no matter how I tried to reassure them of all things that might flatten a day's plans like flat tires, bad weather, or the bird flu, they'd always come up with another Yeah-But. And then another round of What-Ifs. It was maddening at times, and I'd find myself wishing I could spend a day here and there with one of those Why-is-the-sky-blue-kids and take a small respite from the What-if-we-spill-the-grass-seed-and-the-squurriels-get-constipated-kids.

Fast-forward, a couple of decades and my offspring still voice the occasional What-If and blast me with the Yeah-Buts when they don't agree with me. And I let them do their thing now, turning myself into the proverbial bobble-head figure (just smile and nod), because these once-small humans are now "adults" and can't be told their reasoning may be flawed.

Especially by an old woman like me.

And so, I find it's a relaxing outlet to do my own What-Ifs. I ask this of the universe, of politics, and of science. Sometimes the What-Ifs are reasonable and help guide the reality of our day-to-day mundane-ness: Keep the spare aired, take an umbrella, and stock up on the hand sanitizer.

Other times, the What-Ifs are more of the constipated-squirrel variety and spark Little Miss Muse off into a story.

What if the government dictated who qualified as a good parent?

What if someone "out there" designed our environment like a movie set?

What if we *almost* figured out how to reset the planet?

What if we're in our third or fourth life and we *knew* it?

What if we had an AI that would let us hear everything anyone ever typed?

What if signing up to help at the school carnival was the worst decision of your life?

So, it's in honor of those long and glorious days of parenting small kids and the constant barrage of imaginative What-Ifs that I dedicate this first volume of *Out There* to my children—adults numerically, my quirky, blond-haired, imaginative babies always.

Happy reading!

B. A. Paul

PRACTICE

Sherman Peter Pryor is resourceful—and patient. One must be both when dismantling generations of government interference into the sacred family unit. And a little bioengineering never hurt the Pryor's back-alley national security efforts, either.

Sherman Peter Pryor stood at the rickety metal coffee cart in the dim break room. He chose a giraffe-themed swizzle stick from yesterday's leftover junk for the Captain. Captain Horst was as short and stocky as he was clueless, so the giraffes served as a longstanding gag. Small towns such as Walgram had to make do with the resources available. "Stretch" turned 65, and party vibes, treats, and catering would last all week.

Stretching it out.

Captain Horst would likely ride his oaken desk into the grave. Stretching out the days before a new captain would take the reins.

The swizzle disappeared into the black murk, trying its best to incorporate some smoothness, and maybe some taste, into the brew. The add-in of the day, also a party leftover, was pumpkin spice caramel something-or-other. Sherman preferred black coffee. Decaf, at that. But times like these, one had to make do with the resources available.

Sherman pushed the gentle bustle of the station—already muffled behind the cinder block walls—into the back of his mind as he leaned against the door frame and stirred and sipped the lukewarm and too-sweet coffee. He closed his eyes and allowed his mind to do its thing.

Process. Compare. Analyze.

But when nostalgia started digging in, he realized he needed another dose. His injection was wearing off. However, he allowed the nostalgia some wriggle room. For the moment.

Somewhere, some exhausted little mommy had given birth to a brand-new baby boy. One she and her partner had prayed for and waited for, enduring years of parents and in-laws demanding to know when the young—turned not-so-young—couple would make them grandparents. And now, that infant, red and screaming with limbs still tucked tight from months-long in utero is the most important little boy in the world.

Sherman knew that feeling. Elation. Peace. And when the Allotment had fallen his way, he'd been deemed a fit parent.

Somewhere else, some exhausted mother was pulled from her bed at the sound of a knock. A uniformed pair, hats in hands, dished out bad news and condolences. And her only son, dead on the battlefield in a war neither he nor his mother started, is the most important little boy in the world. At least to her. Likely not to the country he served when the same Allotment that allowed her to birth a son deemed him to be unfit. To that entity, as soon as he'd drafted, he'd become a serial number.

Disposable.

Sherman knew that feeling, too. Grief. Loss. Until finally the Pryors put their collective genius together and, well...

The Styrofoam bottom showed through the last of the nasty liquid, and Sherman threw the cup away and headed down the hall to the interrogation room. Shame, really. That this tiny station had only this one room for the witness. No comfy sofas or television sets to occupy him. Only cinder block walls, a one-way glass, and a metal table bolted to the floor and littered with sweets and coloring pages. Like this tiny little witness would ever think to toss a table or the chair he sat on.

Sherman observed the boy through the glass. Curly brown hair. Brown eyes the same shade, clean and clear. No lack of sleep or crying for this lad. Lashes so long that any working New York model would give the last two years of her career for. The tot looked at the walls, up to the ceiling, down to the floor, then directly at the mirror where his reflection no doubt greeted him. Sherman wondered what the boy thought of his own image.

He turned the handle to the door and, dragging a wheeled office chair behind him, sat across from the boy. The boy slid off his metal chair, stood and pointed to the one Sherman sat in.

Sherman traded with him, allowing the boy the cushioned seat that twisted and turned. Sherman took his boot and drug the wheeled chair a little closer to himself, so the pair were knee-to-knee. He showed the boy the lever on the side of the chair, pumping it up so the boy sat taller. The boy smiled.

Sherman sat back and studied him. This little fellow hadn't said a word since he arrived at the station. Captain Horst and a couple of deputies had bribed and begged. Candy, soda, Crayons, and a dusty giraffe toy—pulled from Stretch's windowsill filled with all things reticulated ungulate—all fell short. The metal table held multiple feeble attempts at prompting communication, but the boy remained mute.

He sat up straight and looked Sherman in the face, unphased, the top of his curls level with the top of the chair's back. He wore denim overalls with a faded red shirt underneath. The too-short pant legs rode up his skinny shins. Mismatched socks, one dingy white and one gray-and-red-striped slid into tennis shoes. Still staring at Sherman, the boy wiggled forward so that his knees could bend over the seat's edge, allowing his feet to dangle free. It would be years before his soles could touch the floor from a seat such as this. His right shoelaces, untied, created the only sound in the room as their tips clacked against the base of the chair.

Later, when the rest of the task force showed up, the noise would grow. The bustle of the station would turn to chaos as the "important" ones took over the investigation, barking orders, making calls, storming the five-room building with more manpower than the walls could hold.

Sherman winked at him. The boy tried to wink back, but only managed to squeeze both eyes tight simultaneously.

Sherman smiled.

The boy smiled and nodded. He knew what Sherman wanted. Sherman was confident the boy could withstand what was to come.

They had practiced, after all.

Sherman wheeled the boy's chair to the side, so his massive shoulders blocked the view from the two-way, then back again, in direct view. Several times, Sherman took the boy for a ride like this. To any onlooker, it'd appear him to be playing with the kid. Cheering him up. Having a spot of joy in an otherwise dreary room.

The boy giggled. A soft, timid vocalization. The first utterance the boy had offered to the Walgram precinct. He'd done so well so far.

Even after all the bribery, the tot hadn't even offered up his name. Well, the name the Pryors assigned to him after the first injection took hold.

After the little one could understand a little more.

Hendrix. Strong. Masculine. Sherman's own son's namesake.

The amusement ride continued. Back and forth, the casters on the boy's chair scraping across the concrete floor. On one of these pendulum swings, he reached for the boy's right sleeve, and, using his index finger, raised the cuff of the sleeve to reveal the child's upper arm. A tiny blue Bandaid clung to the skinny arm. Sherman removed it in one quick motion, then spun the boy back into view. The boy didn't flinch. Likely didn't even realize Sherman had stolen his bandage and tucked the blue wad into his own pocket.

A few more swoops and spins of the office chair.

A few more muffled giggles before setting the chair still again.

Then Sherman Peter Pryor handed Hendrix the ratty giraffe from the metal table, put his index finger over his lips, and winked at the most important little boy in the world.

Practice had taken weeks with this one instead of months like the others. They were learning, Sherman's group. The Pryors practiced their own back alley brand of national security like humanity itself depended on it.

Because it did.

The boy tugged on the giraffe's ear. The injection had taken hold weeks ago—about three weeks to the day when the boy was acquired —so he was way too smart for the idle toys and sugary treats.

Way too advanced. In another week he'd be keener than Sherman.

The month after that, if all went well, this child could run the NSA singlehandedly. Once his vocabulary increased, that is.

In only a few weeks, the practice sessions with this young one went from Stage One to Stage Four. Elevating his status over the other males chosen for the project. Elevating him to the most important little boy in the world.

But the world couldn't know this yet. The world as Sherman understood it wasn't ready for the upending of the Allotment and the Unfit laws. It'd taken generations to deviate from the natural order of things to this degree. It's as if the lawmakers practiced for decades on how to make a society miserable. To crumble and bow to authority. Over and over again. Like a championship high-diver. Try. Fail. Flop. Try again. Until dive after dive is a perfect ten.

And dive after dive, the country had taken quite a while to devolve.

It would take generations, likely Hendrix's generation or the one after, to undo the mockery.

With time, the Pryors were sure their tiny tots, fully bio-equipped with the ability to pass the screening tests and outsmart the lawmakers, would prevail.

With time. And patience.

And lots of practice.

Sherman patted the boy on the head again and left him to his silent studying of the room. A quick glance down both hallways showed a slight increase in the station's activity. The muscle was coming. Getting closer.

Coming to take the child, younger by five years than those in previous trials, into custody. To find this wayward soul a permanent home with an Elite family. To survey and blood-test to identify the ingrate who'd been foolish, careless, unfit enough to allow such a commodity as a son to wander off in broad daylight where a kind, traveling detective such as Sherman could stumble upon him. Where the injection and the boy, with all that practice, would do their thing. Together. In perfect harmony.

Sherman hadn't been too keen on the idea of lowering the age bracket. But his partner had been right. Older kids clung to the hopes and dreams of Mommy, Daddy and Fido waiting at home. So, younger and younger the Pryors went, until they found the perfect age.

Old enough to feed themselves—at least fork-to-mouth skills were developed. Old enough to take care of most bathroom duties and rudimentary teeth-brushings. Old enough for a working vocabulary.

But not quite old enough to tie shoelaces.

Or to tie their current predicaments with a fear response.

Boys like this one were harder and harder to come by. Birth control methods and the mandatory visits the Sterilization Clinics demanded—not to mention the hefty government stipends for couples to remain childless—cut the unwanted pregnancies by more than eighty percent. These methods cut down on unfit parents.

And the Allotment, in all its glory, also cut down on fit ones.

Hendrix's family, his biological family five states over, would be DNA-identified. And the mother, father, and all older siblings—there were three—would never be allotted the opportunity to birth another. All would be hauled to their district's nearest Sterilization clinic and, well, Hendrix would be the last of that family line.

Because fit parents would *never* allow a child to wander off. Neither would proper big brothers or sisters.

And the country just can't tolerate the Unfit.

Sherman's great-grandfather saw this coming. The population control. The increased need for monitoring. Security. Smaller populations of people meant smaller armies. Smaller tax income for the higher-ups.

And an ever-shrinking decline in human decency. When you weed out the fit parents with bribes and threats, the passing-down of the Golden Rule becomes harder and harder.

Sherman was glad that vague Golden Rule, ancient as it may be, was beaten into him with a quite hot rod of iron. He felt the swell of the scar on the back of his neck. A permanent reminder that Great-Grandfather was right in all his ways. The Pryors and those they recruited to right this monumental wrong all carried similar marks. Not identical though.

Practice and time taught them that branding their group with a uniform scar was a bad idea.

So was leaving the Bandaid evidence on the recruits. Sherman felt the tiny wad in his pocket and took the five strides down the hall to the men's room, passing the phlebotomist with her plastic bucket of goodies. Ready to draw blood on the boy. To determine his genetic makeup for family of origin and fitness.

In the restroom, Sherman tossed the bandage into the toilet and flushed, watching as it swirled and hugged the edge. He thought he'd have to flush it again, but the final swish of water from the rim sent the wad out of sight.

An officer came in the restroom and Sherman feigned washing his hands.

"Long wait, huh?" The guy tugged at his pants in front of the urinal.

"Yup."

"Good thing you found him. He's in such shock he can't even cry. Poor fella."

"Yup. Poor thing. Hope they find his parents."

"No kidding. Off to the clinic with them. All the way out on the tracks—," the officer continued to mutter.

Sherman shrugged, keeping his eyes on his sudsy hands. Letting the warm water relax the tension that was starting in his wrists. That's where it always starts. The wrists. The clenching of fists inside pockets. The need to roll and pop the bones to keep the fingers loose. To open juice box straws. To tie shoelaces. To prep injections.

He tried to remember as the officer spouted off about duty and parental honor that this poor fellow was just that. One of the masses, brainwashed by years of propaganda to believe the lies and fallacies in logic.

Sherman left the restroom. Two agents in black suits—a man and a woman—entered the boy's waiting area. The Pryors had known they'd send a woman. A mother figure. So they'd practiced with the boy, whose IQ jumped several points by the day, to withstand her sweet ways and offers of comforting hugs just as he'd withstood playing with toys and chowing down on sweets in the interrogation room.

Hendrix was well prepared. Sherman wasn't worried.

At least he'd have a chance to make a difference.

Sherman's own son, deemed unfit through the screenings, never did. Off to war with him. Off to fight so that the fit and the Elite could live their lives in peace. Repopulate the country with only the best and the brightest.

Stretch motioned for Sherman to join him in the office. Sherman obliged. Another suited man, lean, deep-set brown eyes, and a high-and-tight cut, began the informal questions amid a flurry of giraffes.

Tell me how you came upon the child.

Tell me this.

Tell me that.

Sherman recited all the correct answers. All the correct syllables emphasized. All the correct cadences that would be typical in a time such as this.

"This is, what, your third or fourth find?" The agent's fingers whizzed over his device, the screen no doubt filling with a long list of accolades for Detective Sherman Peter Pryor.

Sherman nodded.

"Great work, Detective. Great work." The guy nodded to the Captain, then joined the others down the hall with Hendrix.

Detective.

Sherman had worked hard—well, with the help of the injections, he didn't have to work that hard—to rise to his position. Undercover work. No black suits or fancy hair cuts for him. He was boots-on-the-ground in the homefront war on the Unfit. Find and report the tiniest infraction.

Kid screaming too much? Might be an unfit parent.

Kid taken to a health clinic one too many times? Not enough times?

Too spoiled? Not spoiled enough?

Dirty looks in public? Hand held too tightly? Not tightly enough?

Sherman had been trained to spot all of this, and with the elite government training program, he'd become quite skilled at it. Proven himself. Then, with practice, he'd become even better at protecting as many families from trips to the clinic as possible. Then Great-Grandfather deemed it time to start acquiring children to plant. Children like Hendrix.

Captain Horst sat back in his wooden desk chair and intertwined his fingers behind his head. "Bet you're pretty proud of yourself. This'll get at least a dozen Unfits dealt with—maybe lots more. Stop the line in time, is what I always say."

By that, the Captain was quoting old propaganda. Stop the Unfit in their genetic lines. In time, there'll be no more of them to deal with. This was taught in schools. Passed around at dinner tables, golf courses, and ladies' luncheons.

Sherman nodded. "I just feel sorry for the little guy. I mean, what'll become of him?"

The Captain reached for his own file and tossed it toward Sherman. "The blood scans. Clean as a whistle. Lad'll be one of the lucky ones. Elite family. Best of the best for the little guy."

Sherman scanned the page of results. The injections were performing well. Holding up under the initial screenings. The boy, by the Pryor's testing, was genetically unfit at the ripe old age of four. He'd have been sterilized by his tenth birthday and slotted for the Draft by the time he was 18. Maybe younger depending on the heat overseas.

The bio shots changed all that, though. Masked the DNA markers and boosted the tot's IQ. Smart enough to figure all this out someday.

And smart enough to stop it.

Sherman slid the file back to the Chief. An old-school manila file. The last district did everything digitally. But in Walgram, a county hit hard by the Allotment and one that "necessitated the doubling of

Sterilization Centers," you had to make do with the resources available.

Until the Elite could build it back up.

Brick by brick.

Or until the Pryor's mighty mini army, one master genius at a time, could tear it all down.

Sherman said his goodbyes to Stretch and strode down to Interrogation. The lady agent was dancing the giraffe on the table in front of the boy. The other agents were busy on their devices, flipping screen after screen building their case.

Hendrix still hadn't said a word.

Sherman knelt so he was face to face with the boy. He tousled the brown curls. The boy's lips, thin and pink, gave the tiniest upright twitch. His eyes sparkled, then he blinked both his lids—a two-eyed wink meant for only Sherman. Sherman winked back and patted the tiny legs. The boy bent his right knee up to his chest.

And, like a boss, the kid tied his own shoelaces.

Without one bit of practice.

OMNIAUDIO

Greg Vance wants nothing more than a bright and shiny life with his wife and daughter, but work and time wear all things dull. The fear of his wife stepping out and the not-so-charming boyfriend his daughter has fallen for creates for weary days. When a new piece of tech promises the ability to hear all and respond in gallant efforts, Greg jumps at the opportunity to expand his understanding of the women in his life... and maybe his own existence.

Greg Vance was nothing special and he knew it. He was a paper pusher, digitally speaking. His grandfather was the lead paper pusher at Omni decades before Greg sat in the windowless cubical. His nothing-special father was a hybrid. Half paper. Half digital. Greg pushed only digital files from one cyber-folder to another. One email to another. One text to another.

All day long. All week long. Until months turned into years and years to decades.

All digital.

Not a hint of paper, pulp, or ink anywhere in the building. Unless you count toilet paper, but soon, they'd find a way to digitalize butt wiping.

After each day of digital chaos, he went home to a nothing-special wife. Well, she'd been bright and shiny when they'd first met, but soon, she became stuck in the mundane and routine of her similar desk job and the running of the home. Life ruts rub away bright and shiny real quick. Too bad he couldn't rewire his brain. Fall in love with her all over again. But Amille stopped putting effort into their nothing-special relationship long ago. Why should he waste the energy?

The only thing special in Greg's life was his little girl. His little apple dumpling. The promise that something would sparkle brighter in the future. Their miracle child.

He and Amille couldn't have kids of their own. So they took in a gorgeous green-eyed, freckle-faced Samantha. An orphan after OmniAudio's construction of a new tech tower on the end of town collapsed and killed her parents. Killed lots of kids' dads, but her mother had worked there, too. And no next of kin.

Greg was a family man of OmniAudio, so Sammy had been placed with him. Been with the company for, well, for as long as he could remember. Samantha often asked what "omni" meant, more so the older she got. Greg couldn't tell her. Not that he didn't know, he simply couldn't bring himself to utter the words.

Omni—in the company sense—meant everything. They were everywhere. Sometimes it was scary to think about. Overwhelming. So he didn't think about it and he didn't explain to his adopted daughter that OmniAudio was everywhere. All the time.

Her holographic image flicked above the mini photo projector from the corner of his desk. That time down in the Glades when they took the airboat ride, zooming over mere inches of water at breakneck speeds. He could still hear her shrieks and giggles drown the roar of the boat's fan blades. The image hovered in mid-air a few seconds before disintegrating, tiny blocks and codes of light reassembled into her tenth birthday party when Samantha's goofy best friend threw cake in her face, smearing vanilla and chocolate marbled fudge into her curly red locks. She'd licked the icing right out of her hair.

He tore his focus from the memories and tethered it to the monitor. He pushed a few more files around until the alarm on his watch would finally signal that his chains were free and he could leave OmniAudio for the night. For the weekend. A time clock. Literally.

His granddad had to punch a cardboard slip into a mechanical machine to log his hours. His dad logged in on his computer terminal.

Greg wore his timecard. All the time.

But another ninety minutes and he'd be free for a weekend. Well, free of Omni. Not free from the honey-do's and Daddy-will-yous. Though he didn't mind that last one so much. Time with Samantha would be ticking away quickly now that she was in high school.

He drug his mouse from one corner of the screen to the other. He imagined the cursor arrow to be as tortured with the mundane as he. Did that white pointy devil dream of wandering off the edge of the screen? To explore the uncharted territory, the bonds of technology removed so he could point and click at anything he chose to? Not just numbers and rosters and ledgers...

He clicked on accounts received. Only a few of those. Times are hard on folks. The next series of clicks, after checking his watch for the tenth time, landed on accounts due. Lots of those.

Last was new inventory. That shouldn't take long. OmniAudio wasn't positioned to release the next feat of audio-engineering until—

Wait. He clicked the file closed then opened it again. Refresh the page. Blink. Maybe clear the drear from his eyes.

But there it was. A new line item. Under the category of employee trials only. Not available to the public yet. Oh wow.

Fresh off the conveyor belt.

The OmniAudio Mag 5.4. Small as a mustard seed. Much, much smaller than the wearable earpiece Greg had used his bonus coins for back when he was still courting Amille. He hadn't spent any more coins since then. He could afford a trial run of this new gadget without so much as a feather's brush to their household budget.

Not that Amille would notice. She goes through money the way his daughter goes through guys.

And Samantha had a new guy in her life, and the boyfriend didn't sit well with Greg. Greg knew the kid was much older than Sam, but he didn't know by how much. She was a teenager on hormones and only let out the tiniest trickle of information.

Greg also knew the guy's name. Krank. What kind of upstanding family names their kid Krank?

Previous guys were Jason and Ryan and Camden. She went through those so quickly, it made Greg and Amille's heads spin. They'd met all three of those dudes. Typical pimple-faced high schoolers who tried to make eye contact and give Greg firm handshakes. One even threw in a "yessir" for good measure.

Now "Krank" ends up in dialog and flashing across her screen's home page and hovering above the new desktop projector she'd gotten for Christmas.

His watch signaled quitting time, along with the sound of a dozen other Omni-fites standing, their chairs no doubt spinning and scooting away behind them as they grabbed their belongings and headed for the elevator.

But Greg ignored the alarm and the rush. He stared at the screen. OmniAudio Mag 5.4.

Wow. His had been a 1.9, if he remembered correctly. The size of his grandfather's hearing aid. And it didn't take long for people to catch on that he was wearing it. Eavesdropping. Especially Amille. But he had caught and questioned her about that pathetic loser of a neighbor. Dwight had Greg up in arms ever since he'd taken his Amille for a ride in his new fire engine red convertible.

It had taken Greg nearly nineteen years in this cubical to rack up enough employee bonus coins to try out a new piece of tech. Some of the higher-ups and better-paids earned enough to try a new piece out every couple of years.

With the 5.4, he could listen in, so to speak. The original models had glitches, but by this deep into the version and re-versions, surely they'd worked those out. The automaton narration had been fixed in version 3.3 when OmniAudio added a plethora of choices. Sultry female. Strong, black, and handsome. British. Jamaican. Any flavor and any soul you'd care to hear narrate the digitized information you were in "earshot" of.

Yup. Greg pushed back his chair, and the echo bounced off the vacated cubicles.

Greg headed for the elevator and instead of pushing the well-worn ground level, escape-the-building button, he jabbed at Floor 10's bright and shiny button. Where the new line items and the gurus to install them lived.

Literally. Lived.

They had apartments up there and everything. Top-secret tech and designs guarded under lock and key right down to the poor tortured souls who created such feats.

The door slid open and Greg stepped into a warm, muted reception area. Beige walls. Brown and cream swirled, loopy carpet. Tan leather seating area. Coffee cart. Vanilla bean and espresso hung in the air. Monitors on the wall boasted of OmniAudio's history—even if the only ones to ever see the screens were employees who'd been dutifully indoctrinated on all things Omni. And Greg more than some given that he'd listened to his grandfather's tales of work. And then his father's.

Greg may be the only family man in the joint.

The receptionist smiled at him and blinked. She had a pristine olive complexion without too much makeup. Gorgeous dark eyes. Hair to match. She wore all green. Not that crazy green that Sam insists on. A more subtle, professional shade. Like, well, like olives.

"How may I help you, today, Greg?"

A bit startled that she knew his name, he had to gather himself before he spoke. "Well, I, uh." He cleared his throat. Man, was she gorgeous. "I'd like to cash in my coins. On the new OmniAudio Mag 5.4."

She smiled. "You'll be our first, Greg." Her perfectly manicured hands flew over the keyboard and gave a nod toward the coffee cart. "You can have something while you wait. How are Amille and Samantha?"

Greg stopped mid-stride to the cart. Now that was something. He rarely spoke of his family outside of his two next-door cubical neighbors. He guessed someone could surmise he had a family if they stood and watched his desktop projection frame for any length of time, but Greg knew—he just knew—he'd remember if he'd ever spoken to this, this...

"They're fine. Fine. Say, what's your name?"

Her eyes met his. "Olive. And it's nice to meet you, Mr. Greg Vance."

He stared at her. A bit too long, but he couldn't help it at this point. While he debated on pressing the issue with her or getting a cup of black, the massive oak door Olive guarded opened and a tech, dressed all in robin's egg blue scrubs, blue hairnet, and blue shoe coverings motioned for him to follow.

"This is exciting. Exciting, Greg. I'm so glad. How's work been treating you? Saving up those coins for a while now, huh? How'd you find out—"

The tech fired one question after another at him without giving

Greg a chance to answer one. Way too many trips to the coffee cart. Or way too many days locked up with the same people during the development phase of the Mag 5.4.

The Omni-fites up here likely knew the answers if they monitor the time his cursor spent hovering over the new line item back at his computer station. That's probably how Olive knew. She'd already pulled his personnel file and was waiting on him. OmniAudio was always good at predictions.

"So, have a seat up on the table. This should only take a moment to insert and sync."

Greg obeyed.

The tech rummaged around on a tray and a second, equally blue technician wearing thick, black gloves brought in a smoking canister and sat it on the counter. He screwed the top off and the first tech, using the slimmest and longest tweezers Greg had ever seen, extracted a speck-of-a-something from the midst of the fog rolling over the sides of the container.

"So, whadya think of Olive?" The tech's question threw Greg. Greg was tired of getting thrown. All in the last few hours or so. What was he supposed to say to that?

"Well, I, uh..."

"She's the newest design. Remember Flora?"

It came back in a wave. Flora. The impossible-to-please receptionist of Floor 10 from years ago. When Greg had come to get fitted the first time he'd spent his coins. Flora. Of Floor 10. Greg couldn't do anything right. He and a few of his co-workers had secretly called her a cyborg.

Wait.

Wait a minute.

"Newest design? Really?"

"Yeah. Much, much better than Flora, don't you think?"

Greg resisted the urge to run back to the front waiting area and study Olive's perfectness. Flora had been old and gray with a bun on her head. But he'd had no idea.

"We canned—literally recycled them into cans, I tell ya—Flora, Vail, and Cam. Olive's showing great promise. Great promise."

Greg coached himself to keep it together and at least pretend he knew an inkling of the goings-on in the company he'd given life and blood to for over thirty years. Was it thirty? Good lord, he felt like he'd been born and raised within Omni's walls.

The new line item took him by surprise—and now the smack-you-in-the-face realization that the tech guys must be spending their every waking hour creating reception robots. For decades.

Wow.

"Now hold still. This may pinch. We all have one. They take a bit to get used to, but you can turn the volume up and down, as well as the sensitivity with your watch. Hey, give me your watch, and I'll set it on the lowest so you can get used to it." Before Greg could respond, the skinny metal tweezers disappeared from his peripheral vision into his ear canal, and, if he didn't know any better, he thought he'd been stung by a wasp.

He reached his left hand up instinctively to grab at his ear, but the tech stopped his arm and removed his watch in one smooth motion. "No pressure to the area. No pressure at all. The stinging will stop soon. Give it some time."

Greg slid his hands under his thighs and closed his eyes. The stinging abated, replaced by a tickle and a high-pitched ringing in his ear—but just the left one.

The tech returned his watch, tapped the screen a few more times, then said, "Now see if you can hear this. I'll text Olive."

The tech tapped his own watch, his fingers a blur over the tiny screen.

Hey, Olive. This is Greg's test.

Hey, Will. That's awesome. What a beneficial tool the Mag 5.4 will be for our dear Gregory Vance.

Greg's eyes nearly popped out of his head at the crystal clear text-to-speech. "How is this legal?"

"Oh, anyone using Omni's servers agrees to this. The government's going this way, too. Well, they went this way a long time ago. Oops. TMI. TMI, buddy. Now, don't you go dragging information out of me like that..."

"But like I said, you can dial down the sensitivity, and I have the capability to dial up my 'findability.'" The tech, Will, winked at Greg. "But if I were you, I'd not mention that to your teenager. Or maybe even your wife?" That last line was a jab. He grinned and left the room, leaving Greg to resist digging a finger into his ear to itch the vibrating sensation.

The voices came back. Clear and strong. The program even indicated who was texting.

Do you think this is wise? This one came from Will.

Well. He's got to find out at some point. That was from Olive. *But you may want to tune your findability. He can still hear you.*

OmniAudio knows something.

His company knows Greg wants to spy on his kid.

And maybe even his wife.

Greg played with his Mag 5.4 Friday night and most of Saturday before he found a setting that didn't pick up on everyone's texts for miles around. The first few hours out of the building felt like jet planes roaring their engines in his ear canal. Occasionally, there'd be a clear message he could hear through the jumble.

Bring home milk.

I'll be late. Lots of those.

Who do you think you are, you sick son—

But mostly, the input resembled the whir and buzz of an overly crowded casino. Capital letters came through as shouts. Emojis came through in different dings and tones. Some messages came through in the users' original languages. He'd played around with the sensitivity until he zoned in on only Samantha's.

Then Amille's.

Some of his wife's texts were about work. More than a few vents Amille typed out to a best friend—a guy friend—Greg hadn't realized she'd reconnected with. Bemoaning motherhood to an ungrateful teenager. That made him angry. That she thought of their apple dumpling girl as something to regret.

She bemoaned choosing a nothing-special man. Choosing Greg.

*Maybe I made a mistake. Maybe I could recal—*Greg turned the audio down before he could hear the rest of her text.

Those messages, played in crystal clear clarity through his implant, unknown to his wife. Those messages made him, well. Nothing.

He had not the first feeling about that.

He'd played around with the audio options until he found a dead ringer for Olive's voice. Smooth. Sultry. And he only felt a little bit ashamed. She was an automaton, after all. And Amille, well. Greg was nothing special. He knew it. And his wife did, too.

Saturday night Sam started texting Krank. Krank! How Greg hated that name.

Dad doesn't know. He won't understand. He thinks—

Give it some time. I know Will can help. I've watched him work.

But I don't want to hurt him. He's like a father to me. And Omni, well, they're...

He is your father. He took you in.

Can he be, though? Amille I get. She's, well, she's real. But Dad, Dad's...

Greg is what he is. Floor 10 will help. Trust me. And drop it for now. In case he's online.

K. See you tomorrow. Followed by the happy high-pitched tones of red heart emojis. Four in a row.

Wait. Wait. Greg's mind wheeled back from Floor 10 to the messages playing out loud in his head. Krank knows Will?

Krank? He knows about Floor 10? Only techs and the born-and-bred-die-hard Omnis know about Floor 10. It was protocol. Subject to fines and imprisonment should information leak...

Was Krank the one who delivered the smoking mustard seed? Couldn't be. He's much too old for his Sammy. His Sammy. Not some other person's child. His child.

The one he took in.

Greg is what he is. What the hell was that supposed to mean? And that ingrate's got his little girl believing Greg is something that he's not. Krank!

Weekend or not, Greg took his sorry, nothing-special carcass back to OmniAudio. He refused to wait until Monday to get to the bottom of this.

GREG BEAT THE FLOOR 10 BUTTON AS HARD AS ONE COULD WITH only a thumb. Greg turned his Mag 5.4 to the lowest setting on his way to Omni. He didn't want to pick up stray bits of texts and fighting and flirting and real living. His life was full of chaos—he didn't want to ingest everyone else's.

The elevator slid open.

Olive greeted him. Something inside him felt connected to her, though he'd only seen her that one time. But her voice had been in his head, reading everyone's messages. Making even the awful sound bearable.

Olive smiled. "Greg, what a nice surprise. And on a Saturday."

"I need to see Will."

"Are you having difficulty with your Mag 5.4?"

"No. I'm having difficulty with Will. I think."

"Oh, my." She motioned over the keyboard. "Let me call him out. You can wait, if you'd like." She nodded toward the tan couch.

"No thanks. Olive, is there someone here named Krank?"

Olive's face went blank. She picked up the phone. Slowly. Not breaking eye contact. A pause. "He knows."

"He knows? He knows what?" Greg demanded, forgetting about

her beauty and his inexplicable attraction toward her. "Greg Vance knows what?"

Olive rose calmly from her chair. "Greg Vance knows all. Omni. Omni means all." Her smooth tone froze him. He couldn't move, his feet felt as though they were cast in concrete. His hands went from their angry position on his hips to limp at his side.

He couldn't speak.

It was like he was going into shutdown mode.

Omni means all.

He could still see. Still process input.

Will sprang into the waiting room followed by the other tech. Will called the other tech Krank. "Time for a reboot, Mr. Vance. Amille requested a reboot. You're third generation, a good run, really. Time for an upgrade. Sammy and Amille will be so happy with the recalibration." The techs loaded him onto a dolly and took him to an exam room where another better, brighter version of himself stood in the corner.

Thicker hair. Firmer stature. Taller, even.

Omni means all.

The reboot phrase. His reboot phrase. One that he couldn't say lest he perform a memory wipe on himself. Olive did it for him.

Olive...

Will removed his mustard seed from his left ear canal and placed it in his new body.

Samantha. Would he remember her?

Krank removed another larger chip from deep in his right ear with those same long tweezers.

And all went dark.

Sunday morning the sun shone through the breakfast nook. His wife, his gorgeous, loving wife had made pancakes. His Mag

5.4 indicated that Amille was thrilled with how things are going in their marriage. She'd told her girlfriend from work this. Samantha brought her new boyfriend over for brunch. Krank. What a unique name. And such a pleasant young man. Greg could really get used to having him around.

Greg felt great. Amazing girl. Great wife. His chest swelled. Pride. Satisfaction. Life was sparkling and shiny and full of potential. And Greg felt better than he had in, well, a whole generation.

VIABLES

A clandestine facility decked with the highest level of tech and bioengineering the brightest minds could master. A gallant effort to save a chosen few after the world goes to pot. Has the Directive to save a slice of mankind worked, or will the Architect discover if Freedom Phase is as pleasant as it sounds...

My lids open slowly. Retina-shattering light scorches the backs of my eyes. I close them again, though the synapses linking lids to nerves aren't firing as quickly as I'd like, and the headache starts immediately. I reach a weary hand up to add a thicker layer between me and the ultraviolet rays, my fingers tangling in chest-length beard on their way up.

Sound comes online next. First that of oxygen rushing through my nostrils, entering and leaving from my lungs despite the heaviness in my chest. Then rhythmic waves, as if I'm lying face-up in warm sand on the brightest beach, the ocean a few yards away, lapping and slurping at the shore.

With eyes still sheltered, my other hand feels for the sand beneath me. I grasp for a fistful of grains to let drift through my fingers. To confirm my location. To confirm I've not misunderstood my predicament.

What I grasp isn't sand. It's smooth. Cloth? My legs are heavy, something weighing them down against this fabric. I don't think I'm wearing any shoes.

Confusion ticks up my spine, spurring me to remove my hand from my face and try the eyelids once again. I squint hard before opening, trying to spread as much moisture over my dry eyes as possible before facing the light.

Before facing the truth.

Where did it go? All the moisture? Mouth, eyes. My entire body screams for liquids.

The confusion piles in a panicked heap on top of my chest. The weight from mere seconds ago is heavier now, heavy with a *knowing*.

I don't think I want to know. I don't think I need to confirm.

My memory struggles to grasp that thin edge of reality. A flash sears through my mind, the first clear thought since the bright light. Driving in the fog in my rusty blue Ford pickup. Bumping along the country roads. Dodging potholes. Dodging the deer.

Miscalculating the distance and hitting the deer despite the dodge.

I could only see part of the massive buck through the thick ground cloud, then all of him. All at once. On the windshield. Through the windshield. Hooves. Fur. Blood and broken glass in front of me.

Pam to my right.

It's like that now. Seeing and comprehending only bits of my environment. I know the hazy, heavy reality will reveal itself in a terrifying jolt. Likely with blood and broken glass.

I'm not sure how I know this. I just do.

I will my lids open and face the brightness. Not as bad as a minute ago. Not great, either. My hands are free of the fabric. While my eyes adjust, they explore. Soft cloth, like well-worn cotton. Sheets. The tightly woven edge of a blanket. My coarse beard sprouts from my cheeks and jaw line, falling onto another cottony material of a shirt or gown.

My scalp. The scar from hitting the deer buried deep under long locks. I trace the locks down. Extremely long and tangled in my facial hair. Tubing snakes from my nose, winding its way behind my ears. I pull on this. A hiss of air escapes into the room instead of into my nostrils. I drop the end of the plastic and it tangles in the beard.

I've never had a beard.

I've never had long hair.

With a few more blinks the room emerges from the fog. Above me lights too bright to focus on. In front of me, rather at the tips of my blanket-covered toes, on the wall, a projection of Tahiti or Key West. Palm fronds flap in unfelt breezes in the top left corner. Ocean waves extending from cobalt blue depths lap against the sand. A bright ball of orange guards the top right. The sun. Nice image.

I think I remember picking this one out long ago in another room and in another time still enveloped in fog and not quite attainable. I think Pam was there. I think she picked the same image. We were in this together, after all.

To my left, a split-door, divided at the one-third mark. Bottom closed. Top swung open. A sink. A cabinet.

Another door, unsplit. Open. Toilet and second sink beyond.

One would need moisture to need a toilet. I bring my knees up and position my elbows under me to swing my legs out of bed, and I think I feel a catheter. I don't check though. I don't want to know that yet.

"Please remain supine."

Startled, I lower my legs and turn my head to the right. Drapes, black and pleated, hang from high near the ceiling down to the floor. They cover the whole of the right side of the room. Wall? Window? No light escapes their grasp.

The orange ball above the ocean moves.

"Please remain supine."

The panic turns to dread. I remember this part. From that same hazy room and that same foggy time where I picked the beach image. That voice.

Pam's voice. But not Pam.

The thought of her wrings pain around my rib cage, but I don't have time to process this. The orange light hovers over me. Whispered humming with the rhythm of the waves.

I blink again. Not just light. Metal. Two slices of a silver sphere. An orange ember glow, warm and comforting, seeps from where halves meet. An appendage protrudes from the base of the thing. A thin, gunmetal gray arm with a rounded end aims at my face.

"Please remain supine, Mr. Levine."

I comply because I think that's what I'm supposed to do. I think complying gets me out of the room. Onto my feet. Free of tubes and catheters and away from the black curtains. I think this because I remember the training. I don't know to remember this training willingly, it just...comes.

Foggy, hazy training.

I lie back. Head flat on the bed. Hands at my side. I remember studying for this part. Going through rote memorization of facts.

Lying down and rising from a similar bed and...something else...until muscle memory took over—as my muscles do now.

Pam's voice emits from the flying orb. This gives me comfort. I think that was also an option, as was the scene on the wall. The voice. Programmable to familiarity.

She guides me through the drone, only slightly robotic in tone. Very high quality. Nice job.

I can't quite grasp my predicament, but I know compliance moves the process further along. To when I can see Pam. Hear her true voice. Touch her. Hold her.

As the orb moves toward my head, a green laser spills from the rounded tip. I close my eyes against the glare until it moves toward my neck, and chest. When I can open my eyes, I'm enveloped in a sparkling green grid, glowing, pulsating. I raise my arm, and the grid bends and twists around my hand. I can't touch it, but it moves with me. It doesn't spill onto the blankets or bed. Rather, it wraps and coils to my body, not wasting one micron of energy on the cloth sheets.

The grid is warm, almost too warm, like a heating pad that had been left in the microwave thirty seconds too long. Even through the blankets and my cotton coverings I can feel the squares, one inch by one inch, dancing and bending around me.

All the way through me.

Down toward the bed. Down toward my spine and buttocks.

"Please remain still and supine." Pam knows best.

I drop my hand and watch as the machine, a couple of feet above me now, scans my whole body, head to toe. Then backward from toe to head. The metal arm retracts into the belly of the craft. The orb returns to its rightful place, Earth's only star guarding the vast oceanscape.

Guarding the room.

Guarding me.

Wrapped in the lingering warmth of the dancing grid, I don't worry about the black wall of curtains. Nor the catheter. The overgrowth of hair and beard fades into the foggy recesses.

I am at an uneasy peace. And all I want to do is sleep.

AT SOME POINT DURING MY REST, I TURNED ONTO MY RIGHT side. The black wall of curtains has kept me company. I've no concept of time. No idea if beyond the walls of this facility the stars are awake and twinkling or if they've retreated behind a cloudless azure filament.

I stretch my legs and rub my face as I roll to my back. The oxygen tube is gone. So's the catheter. The sun in the room hovers in the corner, an unobtrusive guard. Keeping one eye on the orange glow and the other on the floor, I aim my feet from under the covers and attempt to stand. I use the bed's edge as a support until the feeling in my soles registers that I have indeed accomplished this task.

More stretching. The pale blue gown dangles at my kneecaps. The orb allows me a few steps then hovers a few feet behind. I stagger to the bathroom and shut the door on the orb. I think, given all I've been through, I deserve a moment to myself.

Reassured that my plumbing is functioning, I flush, wash my hands, and focus above the sink. No mirror. No artwork. Just wall. I'd like to see my face with its new—or rather old—fur covering. I'd like a shower, but there is no stall in this tiny restroom. I open the door.

My orange orb waits for me. Through the top third split in my room's door, two more drones fly in. These are larger by double than the one who speaks to me. They have double appendages. Two triple-jointed spider legs in the same gunmetal gray sprout from their bellies, thicker by inches than my orb's. Stronger. Tri-graspers on the ends, three metal skeleton fingers at the end of each appendage, ready to obey the lead drone's directive.

Tri-graspers. Lead drone. I know these terms, though I'm not entirely sure how.

"It's time for orientation, Mr. Levine."

"Orientation?" My voice is guttural. I almost don't understand my own utterance. I clear my throat. "Orientation?" I've upgraded from guttural to gravel.

"Please sit down, Mr. Levine." Pam's programmed vocalizations sound more stilted now that my head is clearing. I comply and sit on the bed. This orb hangs directly in front of my face, eye to eye if the thing had eyes. The others to my right and left, near the head and foot of the bed.

"Where's Pam?"

"Mr. Levine, please watch the screen."

I twist around to the oceanscape, which pixilates away frame by frame. The lapping of the water and breeze through the fronds goes mute. The white wall glows from behind for a moment, before the images flash. Frame by frame. Some pixelated. Others so clear I believe I could reach out and be wrapped in the scenes as the green grid wrapped itself around my hand.

Some images are from my own photo collection. Pam and I on our first date. The wedding day. My pup, Vince. Shaggy gray mutt dragging a muddy stick from the river's edge. Pam took that shot.

Vacation in Cozumel. Underwater shots, snorkels, and fins. Skiing in Aspen. Snow crunching under our boots.

I reach my hand toward the screen and try to stand. The two large orbs use their tri-graspers, placed gently on each of my shoulders, to stay me in the bed. I drop my hand and comply.

One image every few seconds. Then several a second. Until my orientation is done, and I am now fully aware of my predicament.

I did this.

Pam did this.

This facility.

The images morph from personal and private to the global scale. Riots. Wars. Bombs. Chunk by chunk, the last bit of humanity, all believing they deserved to have whatever they wanted, snuffed out by their own progress. Or lack thereof.

Then the natural disasters, whether God-sent or manmade, in the end, it didn't matter. Some ecosystems thrived—bacteria. Others did not—fowls, fish.

Humans were next.

Pam. The team. Me. We saw it coming. We wanted to put our fingers in the dam before it all fell victim to apocalyptic floods. Save what we could. *Who* we could. A few thousand Viables. Let the rest tank themselves with their stupidity.

The facility would help us do that. In the middle of nowhere shrouded in pines and redwoods and cliffs. Clandestine.

Put technology to the good use of preservation rather than destruction.

"Where's Pam?" I weep as I swallow more gravelly grains in my throat. A high-pitched wail erupts from the depths of my gut. Even as I ask the question, I know where Pam is. She's dead.

I bring my knees up to my chest and fall back into the bed, closing out the screen. The orbs.

The black drapes, unmoving. Unwilling to reveal the true terror of outside.

I gather myself. "Where's everyone else? My team?"

"Some next door." The orange glow brightens as the orb hangs over my head. "Some on other floors. Some are no more."

"Are they awake? Did you bring them out of stasis?" I sit up and wipe the dampness on the corner of a sheet. Two more drones fly through the top third of the door. One with a packet of bed clothes dangling from its hooks, the other with a bag of toiletries.

"Are they awake? The team?" Despite the fresh grief, though not fresh at all, as Pam died the night of the deer. Blood and broken glass. On our way here. To our facility.

I feel my well-healed scar buried deep under long, unruly locks. Not well-healed during my time in the stasis chamber. Healed far before then. Pam's loss grieved well before the chamber. The foggy haze is lifting, and I relive the loss—my fault, I was driving—all over again. I try to compose myself. Someone, somewhere, is watching.

Manning the drones. They must be. The rest of the team must be awake.

"All have been woken. You are the last, per the Directive."

The last one. To wake up. The last Viable.

"Babies? Are there babies?"

My orb, my Pam, remains silent. Hovering and humming. Waiting.

The cleaner drones urge me to stand. They remove my clothing and shave my head and my face, locks and beard fall into the hospital gown at my feet. One bot scoops up the mess. The other scrubs me down then drapes a fresh gown over me. The guard bots guard, appendages at the ready. One at the door. One at the black curtain. A synchronized team. Pam, my Pam, the living breathing one, did nice work.

"I demand an answer. Are there children? Another generation?" I was slotted to be woken last. Per the Directive. Per our carefully architected methods.

Pam and I couldn't have kids. A result of the decline in the genetic pool. Drugs and advanced weapons and depleted nutrients in food. We were not Viables. Not really. We were valuable to the program, however. As Originators and Architects, we were saved.

Well, I was saved. Pam didn't live to see her own success.

Blood and broken glass. I shake the memory.

I've been sleeping for a century. Slumbering in a life-preserving chamber. Watched over by drones and AI machines. Meticulously cared for and, when necessary, resuscitated.

"The Directive has failed, Mr. Levine." Pam's voice didn't falter. The more she tells me, the more she reveals, the more robotic she becomes. The less comforting the orange glow oozing from her midsection. "We've moved to Freedom Phase."

My legs give, starting at the hips. The bouncer bots sense this and grasp me under my shoulders, ushering me back to the bed, their metal digits digging into my armpits. My head swims, confusion in a foot race with dread and despair.

The cleaner drones leave through the split door. My orb floats above my head, her middle glowing orange, her appendage glowing green, and she drenches my misery with one-inch-by-one-inch flickering squares.

Then all goes as black as the drapes.

WHEN I WAKE, MY BEARD HAS SPROUTED, AND MY ROOM IS silent. Days? Weeks? My hair isn't nearly as long as it was when I'd first seen this room. The scar runs deep along my scalp line. But I'm okay with this. What happened, happened. The wall at my feet is cold and white. All drones have left me.

I'm not foggy or hazy-headed. I'm not fearful.

Resolute. That would be the term. I think the green grid has something to do with that. Pam's idea. Massive amount of programming went into that AI-human interface.

Not depressed. Not anxious.

Resolute.

We tried. We failed.

I swing my feet out of bed. A wheeled table draped in white linen with a sterling silver service waits for me by the split door. I know the door is locked—both upper and lower parts. I'll be alone from here on out. This part was my plan. I'd been placed in charge of the end of all things, should our Directive fail.

Try as we might, we couldn't get the hovering drones to tackle this task. Doing so would mean they'd bring harm to humans. Which was their number one directive. Do no harm.

So that job was up to me. We'd run scenario after scenario. None were ideal.

The Freedom Phase was the best we could do.

And I remember the black curtains now. I picked out the fabric, heavy wool with black UV-proof backings. Thick. I remember how excited the young woman had been on the phone when I'd placed our order. Enough for thousands of windows. Large windows. I wonder now what became of the gal on the phone. Excited, likely earned a huge commission from my purchase. Was she phased out with the population control? Caught in an explosion? At any rate, she'd not been picked for our project, and she's been gone forever.

Though not as long as Pam.

I lift the lid of the silver service and smile. Spaghetti steams under rich red marinara, tiny bits of beef sprinkled on top. Tiny bits of cheese. I know it's rehydrated, but man, does it look like it came from the finest Italian restaurant. A green salad and caramel cheesecake accompany the main course. I replace the lid.

If Pam had made it this far, and the Directive failed, her meal would've been fried chicken, mashed potatoes, and lime Jell-O.

I smile. If the Directive had worked, and Pam had lived, and we'd made it this far, the meals would've been the same. Chosen decades ago, freeze-dried, and preserved for this long. Drones programmed with serving directions for each Viable's meal—whether celebratory or final.

I face the black curtains. In the corner where the sun had shone above the ocean stands a metal pole. By the looks of it, given the layout of the room, it could be an IV pole, waiting to hold bags of life-giving fluids and medication. But this one was not. There were no hooks for saline drips. There were no wing-nuts waiting to secure dosing units or morphine pumps. It was just a pole with four rubber-covered black prongs at the bottom for stabilization.

At the top, the metal tapered to a point. I reach up and touch the tip.

It'll do the trick. Nice job.

I decide, nice as the meal looks, that I'll skip it. Resolved to get on with the final phase. I pull the curtains open. Had this been any other building, or in any other home, I'd have expected a cloud of dust particles to swirl around my head, but the cleaning bots had done their jobs well. The drapes were crisp and clean and had held up well. Likely hadn't been opened all the way in decades, because what would a drone do with a view?

The sun, the real sun, shines above. It's whiter than I remember. The sky isn't as blue as I'd hoped. Not as blue as my oceanscape scene allowed me to believe it could be, anyway. I look to the left and right. The facility is so large, I can see walls of windows extending in either direction. In front and below me, the narrowest of land ledges, not much wider than a New York City sidewalk, wraps around the bottom of the facility. No one has entered or left this building since the program initiated.

No one ever will.

I must be forty stories up, if I remember correctly. Any lower, and we'd have issues with the Freedom Phase. Beyond the ledge, a jagged cliff face tumbles down to the rocky shoreline.

I stretch my arms above my head and lean against the glass pane, looking past my room's windows to those of other rooms. Some are broken, black curtains whipping around jagged glass in and out of the wind. Catching, tearing, trying to retreat to the comfort of the room where their occupants once stared at various landscapes flickering on the walls. Where last meals were eaten—or not.

I look down to the ledge of rocks and shrubs at the base of the building. I spot a few dots of hospital gowns down there. Most cleared the ledge, though. Occasionally, if I hold my head just right, I can catch the shining glittering of glass at the bottom, some amid the shrubs. Some mixed in with the rocks.

I wonder how much glass the ocean tides have carried away. I wonder if the ocean still has tides.

Three times since standing here, I hear clamorings from neighboring rooms. One down the side. Two from above me. I see rainfalls of shards. One pole went flying, gravity and momentum sending the metal spear far into the crashing waves.

And I stand at the window and watch as other Viables execute the Freedom Phase.

My time has come. I grip the pole. I take a few steps back, and using the pole as a battering ram, I shatter the glass barrier. I hold on to the metal pipe and replace it next to the dangling black drape. I think the ocean must have had its fill of these claw-footed objects.

The crisp air sends gooseflesh all around my skin. Somehow, it's more comforting than the green dancing examination grid. I wonder what season this is. I wonder if Earth still has seasons.

I step onto the windowsill, resolved, my gown dancing at my kneecaps. I step into the air.

I'd known when I'd first awoke hours ago—days ago?—that memories would likely come back in jolts. In sprays of blood and broken glass.

And that's how I'll lay my memories to rest.

ON THE FENCE

Throughout multiple millennium, Roger Munsen has seen it all. And each time he must choose his own fate. It's just another day, just another apocalypse.

A fter three apocalypses and one police chase through what used to be old downtown Chicago, Roger Munsen knew better than to jump a fence when fleeing danger. Or climb a wall. Or dive, roll, duck, or tuck under any sort of barricade where the opposite side was, well, sight-unseen and terrors-unknown.

Nevertheless, the drive for survival trumped his millennias-long experience with such things and, this being at least his fourth apocalypse and likely not his last, he decided to scale the crumbling stone wall using the hollows left behind by missing stones as toe and finger holds, then sat down atop the seven-foot structure as if riding a horse. The wall was about as wide as his first mare from eons back. How he missed that horse...

Facing east, legs dangling on either side of the wall, he stilled his breathing and paused. Not pausing had been his mistake all those other times—well, lack of pause paired with the thinner and more slicing nature of barbed wire fencing or fangs or clouds of spores of this, that, or the other. Had the end not been so near, this pause would be refreshing. The azure sky with happy little fluff balls seemed to mock his predicament.

The gathering smoke and spewing ash would show that sky a thing or two.

Skies shouldn't be so fat, dumb, and happy at the end of the world. A warm spring breeze drifted over the distant trees, dancing their green wigs in peaceful harmony. Only the faintest smell of burning wood dotted the wind. That would change. Was changing the more the lava claimed.

This whole landscape would change in a matter of hours. Maybe that's why the sky is happy for the time being. At least over the forest if not up the mountain. It knows what's about to come is yet another planetary reset.

Pauses are nice, and Roger wished he'd paused in times past. To appreciate the fact that when he was gone from this world, that this world really did spin on. Or regenerate. Or be born again. Something.

Some ray of hope in the pause. That's what he told himself as he shifted his leather pack off his shoulders and to the front of him. He tucked it tight between his legs and caught his breath.

Not that he'd exactly had to outrun the terror on the one side of the wall. But slow-moving terror, is, nonetheless, terrifying and drains one of good sensibilities.

He contemplated the route that led him to this barricade. His left leg, if left dangling, would be consumed in a fiery blaze when the approaching lava reached the wall and began to reclaim the rocks mere humans had the audacity to employ to their protection. A few other humans who lived closer to the base of the volcano ran faster, and, scared like him (even all his practice couldn't retrain that fear center in the brain) had scaled the wall, jumped to the other side and ran or limped away, clinging to each other and a few meager possessions. One poor soul tossed his cocker spaniel over the wall. The dog made it fine, landed like a cat to no ill effect. But Roger heard the owner's ankle snap from his perch and knew the end would be quick for the man once the whatevers-they-are showed themselves from the forest's dark.

Roger wondered if the spaniel would guard and protect against the threats to his owner or simply flee. Spaniels don't likely take pauses to figure out such things during an apocalypse—whether it's their first one or not.

He dug out his canteen from his pack and swallowed the last of his water and ale mix. He'd told himself he'd save that last bottle for the end he knew was coming, but old man Smithers stayed behind in his home and Roger'd poured the guy out most of the booze to calm what would be the last moments of the old guy's life. One last act of kindness. Go out on a high note.

He allowed the empty canteen to clatter down the lava side of the wall. He'd not need to refill it once his pause was complete. He'd not need his pack, either, but experience told him the human condition was programmed to hang onto something, anything—no matter how trivial or useless. So he'd keep the pack with him. His father'd given it to him. The only thing Roger'd packed was the canteen. No need for anything else.

Roger contemplated possible escape routes. His raging pheromones and salty sweat would surely bring out of the forest's rim whatever carnivorous beasts lurked there that caused reasonably intelligent human beings to build the wall in the first place. An entire village had barricaded itself off from the woods, gambling that a mountain with a bad case of heartburn was worth the odds rather than the fanged things.

Fanged things that would leave his right leg, if left dangling, a tiny appetizer—or given the number of people who'd already stamped into the forest to escape the lava, the cherry on top of the dessert.

He froze, paused, not breathing for a few seconds.

Yup.

Judging by the shrieks that all-too-giddy little breeze escorted to the wall, more than likely, he'd be dessert.

Funny thing, when Roger was about twenty-five he realized this wall, built decades before he was born, would be a place to contemplate the end of the world should one come during his lifetime. As a youngster in the foothill village, he'd had a decent time of it. Oblivious. Chubby. Happy. Loved.

About eighteen he realized he'd been here before. Earth or something like it. Multiple times before. And just at the verge of the apocalyptic reset or some near-human erasure. Maybe it was the Powers That Be who'd programmed his brain not to remember until he was older. Each lifetime giving him a decent childhood. A chance to love and be loved.

And have a dog or two.

And a horse. Goodness, how he missed that mare...

A couple of gals, and his very persistent mother, insisted that Roger marry. Have children. A full, wonderful, appropriate life.

But Roger knew what was coming this time. He'd had practice. He'd been on the fence the time before, so to speak, and allowed his heart to trump his good reason and took a wife, deciding himself that surely the cosmos wouldn't continue to slap him into end-of-world scenarios. Small blessing they'd had no children with all the running and dodging and barricade jumping they'd had to do.

A child or infant in those instances would've, well... Roger guessed it would've all ended the same way, but more heart wrenching.

This time, he'd paused, something itching at him from the deepest part of his brain. The part that knew the end would come and Roger'd be responsible for himself and whomever he let into his life.

So he'd paused when Sarah brushed his hand that day in the field as she'd brought fresh water from the brook to fill the hands' canteens. He brushed her off, and his mother thought him of other persuasions. So she, kind, accepting mother she was, had sent Henry round. Roger brushed him off as quickly.

How could he tell these people he knew what was to become of them? Of himself? Come right out and say it? "No, Mother, not interested in love. I've been 'round this mountain before. And so have you and so has Sarah and Henry and all the others before us. Y'all just don't remember like I do."

Well, Roger wondered if Phillip remembered. He seemed much older and wiser than his years. Way too careful and frugal and calculated than any twenty-year-old he'd ever met in any lifetime. Or maybe Roger just paid more attention to the kid, Phillip's red hair pulling attention in a village full of blonds and brunettes. Phillip was a prime choice for a mate, but he'd brushed off as many suitors as Roger had.

Phillip may know...

No. Roger'd never said anything. How could he? Those who squawk of such things get medicated in some millennia. Locked up in others. Lynched, even, depending on the level of societal sophistication.

Nope. Let them live in happy oblivion. Remove those on-the-fence moments from their consciousnesses. Marry or not? Children or not? Farm to hoard food or nine-to-five to hoard weapons or gold? Prepare for lava or fangs?

More people scaled the wall—mostly from the lava's side to the forest's side, though in the time he'd taken to pause and catch his breath, some poor blokes decided lava to be friendlier than dark forests and had scurried up the border a second time in the opposite direction. Confusion, fear, and terror driving them for one more second of survival.

Holding onto hope, and the wall being in the middle of it all.

Roger'd seen that many times. He and his one wife had escaped a band of looters back in LA one time around. Jumped a tarp-covered fence where she'd met her end with a rabid dog and Roger'd not been long behind.

The police chase ended similarly. Flee the good guys and land in a much worse guy's lair. And so Roger'd decided to live decently the next time 'round instead of being one of the looters or one of the worse guys. No one profits in an apocalypse, so may as well spread some positivity.

Not many paused on top of the wall. A few older ones, when they'd reached the stones and realized they were of no physique to deal with a climb, had turned and faced the lava. Resigned.

Some held hands. Some embraced. Some faced it alone. Roger knew a few couples back in the village who'd simply stayed when the mountain started grumbling its last warning. No running or ducking or tucking away at all. They'd known. Either from wisdom of a single lifetime or from this being their second or third or twentieth apocalypse.

It was over quickly. But not quick enough. The smell was getting to him from that left side of the fence. The right side was noisy. At least there wasn't a smell from that direction. Yet.

Sometimes the previous memories crashed into his current circumstances and he had a difficult time separating out the eras. He'd told his mother, this lifetime's mother, he wished he'd had a cell phone. She thought him on the sauce. No such thing existed here. Not during this timeline.

Not yet. And judging by the temperature and screams, not until or unless those glorious Powers That Be reset the universe.

As the sky darkened with ash and smoke, choking out the blue, Roger heard a shuffle behind him and a "Hey, brother."

Roger had no brothers, but that was the typical greeting among the men in his village. "Hey brother," Roger said back as he looked back. Red-headed Phillip straddled the wall about five feet behind him.

"What'll it be this time?"

This time. Phillip did know.

"I was thinking forest. I'm not a fan of the heat."

"Me either, brother."

Roger readjusted his pack onto his shoulders and swung his left leg away from the encroaching lava to meet his right leg. Maybe the beasts were filled up for the moment, and he and Phillip would be afforded another moment or two to reflect.

More shrieks tumbled from the trees and bounced off the wall.

Maybe not.

The heat radiated up his back, wrapping him in one last earthly hug—albeit liken to a hug from one of those awful smelling aunts at family gatherings—before he hopped down. No longer on the fence about burn or be eaten. Roger was glad to have taken the pause to reflect. Maybe in the next reset, he'll be more prepared.

At least he'd not be alone. Phillip had jumped down with him, his own leather satchel dangling from his left shoulder.

"Watchya got in your pack? Sweeties? Ale?" Roger asked.

"Nothin'. Left it all with my nan this time. It'd do me no good and I know it. But she don't know nothin' so she may as well chew taffy as the world burns."

Smart kid. "How many does this make you?" Roger leaned against the wall, pausing again. "It's my fourth. That I remember."

"I remember four others. My fifth."

"Any regrets?"

"Fewer than the last time."

"Yeah. Takes a while to get it through the thick skulls, don't it?"

Phillip nodded and left his pack leaning on the wall. Roger did the same and stretched out the kinks from his pause.

The men faced the forest. "See you 'round?" Phillip asked.

Roger thought about this as the screams popcorned from the forest and the burning stench rolled over the wall. Maybe a war buddy'd not be a bad idea. Someone who understood the ins and outs of the ends of the worlds. Someone who'd taken time to be on the fence and was as resolute as Roger was in how it would all go. "Yeah, Phillip. Look me up. We'll try it together next time?"

Phillip nodded. "Sure, brother."

And with that, the men, no need for goodbyes of the crying sort, strode into the forest to face their resets.

Maybe Roger had lived a good enough life this cycle to earn a chance at another horse. Goodness, how he missed that mare...

HINDSIGHT

Signing up early for the school carnival should've afforded Rea Callahan the upper edge—a shot at a task far more enjoyable than scraping cotton candy cemented to the gymnasium floor and scrubbing toilets. But you don't know what you don't know, and even the most benign of volunteer positions can turn into flaming regrets.

I don't usually have regrets. I worked hard through school and graduated in the top ten percent of my college class. Opened my own brokerage firm. I've put quality time in with my family and I've reaped quality and fabulous memories in return. Some would say I should regret choosing Tray, the father of my children who up and left the three of us years ago, so perhaps I should bemoan my choice in a mate. But I don't. Because that would mean Josey and Quinn wouldn't exist.

And I certainly, not for one second, regret any choice that led to my children being born. And I don't regret the sacrifices made on their behalf. Not for one second.

But as I look at the smoke gray concrete block walls on all sides of me, and as I shift in the cold metal chair bolted to the floor and rest my forearms on the cold steel table—also bolted to the floor—and as I glance at the small black rectangle with its round glass lens glaring at my face from high in the corner, its red dot blinking, a computer somewhere recording each moment in this room, I *do* regret the two seconds it took me to sign my name to the volunteer sheet for the Fishers Elementary School Carnival.

The windowless door opens and a middle-aged man in standard Fishers detective attire enters the room. Another detective. There've been several over the last few hours. This one's fresh and fit. The others who've grilled me were tired and already worn out before my ordeal drug them from their desks or patrol cars. "Rea Callahan?" he asks.

I nod.

"Are you ready to tell me what happened?"

"Where are my kids?"

"They're safe."

"What about that, that *thing?*" I feel my composure slipping away. I fight back tears.

He slides onto the corner of the table. His suit jacket opens, his service weapon hangs from his belt. "Let's worry about getting your statement."

"I've already told you guys what happened." I brush away a stray tear that refuses to stay behind my eyelid. At least I'm not bolted to the table.

Or in a straitjacket.

"Well, you've not told me. And you've had some time to calm down now. So how about we take it from the top?"

Calmed down? No doubt the entire police force believes me to be some bewildered, anxiety-ridden, off-her-meds female. That would make their lives easier, I suppose. The truth, though? Well, I don't even believe the truth.

"If you want the whole story, you'll be more comfortable in a chair." I'm tired and my response is snotty, I know. But, truthfully, I don't want this man in my space. On my side of this table.

The detective nods at the camera.

I inhale a shaky breath, not quite understanding what that nod was about. Another officer opens the door, dragging in a second chair, and sets two bottles of water on the table. The detective moves opposite me into the chair and unscrews his cap. I hear the snap when the plastic seal breaks. He takes several long draws from the bottle and sets it on the table.

I let my shoulders relax. I unscrew my top smoothly. Someone must've figured this weak, delusional female needed her cap loosened. My hands shake. Maybe they're right.

I take a sip.

"Whenever you're ready, Mrs. Callahan."

I close my eyes and remember when the nightmare began.

It began with dragging a cheap ballpoint pen across Sally Buchanan's clipboarded sign-up sheet.

The most regrettable two seconds of my entire life.

"JUST SIGN YOUR NAME ANYWHERE, REA. YOU GET PICK OF THE crop." I remember thinking Sally Buchanan would be better served as a license branch teller rather than the elementary school's PTO board. "Everyone must take a spot. When we all pitch in, we make light work for the whole group." She smiled. A fake smile.

I'm not sure any parent had ever *wanted* to volunteer in the twenty years the school'd put on the carnival. But every PTO leader, whether Sally or some other uppity mother, had a way of guilt-tripping the masses into indentured volunteer-hood.

I scanned the list of available spots—several of which I'd tried in past years. Set-up crews had no clue where to put anything or who was really in charge and it took much longer than necessary. The concession booth was awful. Cotton candy machines caked with layers of sugar were nearly impossible to clean. The clean-up crew had a hard time with that same sugary mess—and more—stuck to the floors, doors, and walls. Last year, I'd spent three hours past the end of the event scrubbing bathrooms after children consumed way too much sugar way too fast.

This year, I'd gotten to Sally early before the simpler, less time-intensive jobs filled up. The prize booth was open. Wide open. I scrawled my name on the line feeling triumphant. Like I scored the winning basket in the county tourney. Sally gave me a list of sources to gather prizes from, the theme of the carnival, as well as my budget. Shopping was certainly more appealing than scrubbing toilets.

I took the list home and scoured the straight-from-China websites for all things kid-friendly and matching the Dino Day theme. I ordered the standard, must-haves for any kids' event: bouncy balls, slime in oranges and lime greens to throw against the wall and watch as it crawled down like an amoeba, foam glider planes (some shaped as pterodactyls, three dozen of those), drawstring backpacks, and other such items for the older kids who thought the carnival to be beneath their elevated, mature statures.

For more specific themed-based items, I chose plush dinosaur critters, tie-on dino tails, dino-printed notebooks and pencils.

And then I saw the eggs.

On clearance, even.

Dinosaur eggs. Five trays of twenty eggs in all colors from natural tones to neon brights. Put the golf-ball sized egg in water and the shell dissolved, revealing a tiny, flesh-colored, lima-bean sized dino figurine. Tiny little spongy things that soak up water and grow to five-hundred times their size in a few days—if you keep the water fresh.

I even planned on sacrificing a few eggs to generate buzz for this great find. I'd break one egg open and mark it day one. The second display would be a dino that I'd soaked for one day. The third and fourth parts of the display would show how the dino grew and grew the longer you let them soak.

The kids would love it.

I knew this because I'd shown the prize selections to Josey, my eight-year-old daughter, and Quinn, my eleven-year-old son, before hitting the "complete order" button. If my test audience consisting of a diva princess and sports-loving boy approved, then I figured I hit the happy medium with prize selection. And they especially loved the eggs.

And they loved the fact that I promised they could keep the display when I was done.

I'd almost forgotten about the carnival in the couple of weeks that followed. There was nothing more to do on my part until the prizes shipped and had to be sorted according to perceived value. The kids had earned points all year for A's and B's and good behavior. Other carnival games would also give out points, and the kids could spend these at the prize table.

I was at work when I got the email that my packages had been delivered. I closed my brokerage firm early and drove home. It was raining that day. It was a Wednesday. One-and-a-half weeks before the carnival—and I wouldn't have time to reorder prizes if they were ruined sitting out in the rain.

Boxes large and tall and light and heavy lined the porch. I wrestled them into the entryway and didn't even consider opening them. I'd wait for Josey and Quinn to get home from school and they could help sort. Or play in the packaging. Some kids don't outgrow the allure of empty cardboard boxes.

I started dinner. My phone kept ringing, some unidentifiable number, and all variations of it. So, I blocked and declined the calls as best I could, chalked it up to telemarketers and my cell number falling off the "do not call" registry, and went on with the night. The calls became so annoying I eventually turned the ringer off. No one ever left a voice mail.

I didn't know I should've answered.

You don't know what you don't know.

I should've answered.

Another regrettable action.

"Can I have a break? I'm not feeling well."

"Mrs. Callahan. We've only barely begun."

I stare at the man across from me. I look at the water bottle, of which I downed the entirety of while going through the intro material. Stress gives me cotton mouth. He sighs, stands, and points at the door. I stand and stretch. He accompanies me a few steps down the hall, has me wait as he ducks his head in the ladies' room, then and stands outside while I enter. I feel like those witnesses in the procedural dramas.

Or a flight risk.

Maybe that's an idea. Fleeing. But I don't know where my kids are.

I'm unsure if I'm just a witness or if I did something wrong. I don't think anyone else knows how to classify me, either.

I splash water on my face. My hair is falling out of the ponytail for the tenth time today. I wrap it back up tight and dry off with rough brown paper towel. Rough and brown like the shell of the egg that started this whole mess.

Actually, that regrettable signature started this whole mess. If anyone but myself had signed up to run prizes, maybe that egg would've stayed in a Chinese warehouse somewhere.

A sharp knock and muffled "Mrs. Callahan" urge my feet toward the door. Back down the hall. Back to the gray concrete room with its lurking camera and detective.

My water bottle had been replaced. Or refilled. I'm not sure which. The sight of two bananas and peanut butter and crackers caused my stomach to gurgle. I'm unsure of the time. Or when I last ate. Or when my kids last ate.

"I'd really like to talk with my children before we go on."

"That's not possible, ma'am. They are safe. I assure you. Let's continue. And try to get as detailed as you can. Even things you don't think are important. Let's see. You were ignoring phone calls and cooking dinner...," he prompted.

I slide onto the hard seat as I reach for a banana and free it from its peel. The sweet smell makes my mouth water, and I'm not even a huge fan of bananas.

I look at the man across from me. I'm not a huge fan of him, either. He turns toward the camera above his right shoulder.

His left ear has a hearing device tucked into the canal.

I hadn't noticed it before. None of the other detectives had one, I'm sure, because they used walkies to communicate. But then again, I wasn't in a "calmed down" state when I spoke with the other officers.

He turns back to me, his green eyes piercing mine, and tips his head to the left, ever so slightly. I probably wasn't supposed to notice his flesh-colored, lima-bean sized earpiece.

I look down at my fruit and begin again.

The kids and I ate dinner that night before homework then the grand opening of the boxes. Josey oversaw taking the packaging off all of the individually wrapped items, and Quinn was in charge of organizing them from smallest to largest so we could assign point values. He also assembled a couple of the pterodactyl gliders for display.

We left the dinosaur eggs for last.

Once the notebooks and pencils and backpacks were all organized and labeled, we turned to the trays of eggs.

We opened the lids—like egg carton lids only bigger—and chose five eggs to be used as the display pieces. We couldn't soak the dinosaur eggs until closer to carnival time, but we needed to pack the bulk of the items up and take them to the school so we could have our living room back. I let Josey choose two—she picked a hot pink one and a speckled purple. Quinn chose a neutral tan and a plain white for his, reasoning that we leave the brighter colors for the carnival kids to pick from.

I chose the last egg. Like Quinn, I found what I thought was the ugliest one, thinking that the prettier, brighter eggs would be more appealing as prizes. Mine was slightly off form. A little rough. Darker brown than any of the others.

That should've been my first clue.

But you don't know what you don't know. Until you have hindsight.

We set our five demo eggs inside the fruit bowl on the dining room table for safe keeping. I marked on the fridge calendar the day we'd start the soaking and dino-growing. Five days before the carnival.

Again, life went on. School, baseball practice, a movie at the theater with Grandma and Grandpa.

More phone calls from unknown numbers. Some looked to be foreign. Asian. Sometimes several an hour. I'd called my wireless carrier and complained. They said to answer it and request no more calls. I didn't listen. I was afraid if I answered it, whoever was calling would sell my number off to more fools who'd never give me peace.

Monday evening came, the Monday before Dino Day, Josey was about to burst with excitement to crack open her purple speckled egg and start soaking the other four. Quinn gave in and let his sister dip his into the water, too.

And I handed her that rough, brown egg.

We gently broke the shell of the first egg and a tiny triceratops fell onto the counter. Josey squealed, high pitched, happy giggles that caused Quinn to complain and hold his ears. "Don't get it wet. That's the first display piece. Go put it on the table." Josey took the pieces of egg and the micro triceratops to the dining room.

Quinn and I filled four glasses with warm water and lined them against the backsplash. Josey crawled onto the countertop and gently dropped each remaining egg into a glass.

"Now what?" She stared at the line of eggs sinking to the bottom of the glasses.

"Now tomorrow, the shells should be all dissolved. We'll remove the dino from the first glass and change out the water on the last three."

We had dinner. The kids went off to homework and I went off to my home office to catch up on paperwork. I returned to the kitchen before bed to run the dishwasher and turn off the lights. That's when I noticed that the brown egg wasn't behaving like the rest.

"Behaving like the rest? How so?"

His interruption startled me. I glanced up to the camera, still blinking red. I glanced down to the table, still holding one banana and some crackers. My water bottle was empty again. I don't even remember drinking.

"Well, the other eggs' water was murky and colored with the dye from the dissolving shells. The brown egg wasn't doing anything."

"So it wasn't behaving, it was just…"

"I thought it wasn't working. That maybe the water temperature was off, or that it was a dud."

"So what did you do?"

"Nothing. I went to bed."

"This didn't worry you?"

"After all that's happened today, *this* is the part of the story that you're hung up on? I'm a single mom of two. I work full time. A non-dissolving child's toy egg wasn't exactly on the top of my worry-about-it list." I feel my face flushing. "I want to see my kids."

"After the statement is recorded, Rea. And it will go faster if you cooperate."

"I am cooperating. I'm telling this in great detail for the hundredth time. I'm drinking your water and eating your bananas and I've stayed seated—which is a major miracle given how sore my rear end is becoming—and I'm cooperating."

He raises his hands and is about to interrupt my rant but I continue. "And it's Mrs. Callahan to you. Only friends and family call me Rea." I stand and pace at the back of the windowless room. He doesn't seem to mind, and he glances at the camera and nods again. Man, I'd love to know how big my audience is.

They may be sending this out to go viral. I begin to feel dizzy just as the other officer brings yet another water bottle. He removes the spent, browning peel and leaves the room.

"Do you need another restroom break?"

I look at his bottle; he's still on his first one. "Do you?" I snark back.

"Continue, please." He motions for me to take a seat.

"I'll stand for this bit, if you don't mind." I take the cap off the fresh bottle. They'd opened it for me again. I pace and sip. The water is cool against my rising core temperature. I can feel the trickle all the way down my esophagus.

He nods and moves to the edge of the table, one hip resting on the edge, leg dangling. One leg on the floor supporting the rest of his weight. I guess if I go off, he's that much closer to a standing position.

"Tuesday morning the kids were excited to see the dinos in the first three glasses. Another triceratops, one I don't know the name of, and a T-rex. We removed the tri and replaced the water in the last three glasses. Quinn wanted to start over with another egg in the last one, but we'd already lugged all the prizes to the school the week before. So we left it and went on with our day."

"Went on with your day? So now you have two soaking figurines and the brown egg which is doing..."

"Doing nothing. Soaking." I get brave and reach around the detective, who doesn't flinch, to grab a handful of crackers. He has the slightest hint of cologne, but the peanut butter trumps it. I munch and pace and sip.

"Were there other eggs like the brown one that's 'doing nothing?'"

"You're asking me if in one of the five trays of toy dino eggs there could have been others that did what my brown egg did?" I take a big swig of water to wash down the peanut butter. And to pause before I rip this idiot's head off. "Well, gee, Detective, I don't know. It's possible my boy and I may have missed other ugly eggs. You'd better get your people on it right away before this whole police station—and the hospital—is full up of crazy people who couldn't possibly have seen what they saw."

I take a few steps closer to him. Much closer. "But if you're implying I've been negligent regarding the safety of other families in this community—and my very own children—you're gravely mistaken. Do I need a lawyer?"

He flinches. A micro flinch, but he flinches. He raises his left hand and stops his fingers a few inches from his ear, lowers his hand, then backs away from me to his seat.

"Mrs. Callahan, please sit. You're not under investigation. We're just doing due diligence here. Please continue, and I'll do my best not to interrupt." He takes the remaining banana and begins peeling it slowly.

I slide back onto the metallic chair, clearly my only supportive ally in the room, and continue.

———

On Wednesday we removed the second soaking toy, and yesterday—was it yesterday? —the T-Rex came out. Still nothing was going on with the brown egg. This morning, Quinn asked if he could keep the "unhatched" egg as part of his rock collection. Maybe it was a geode. Or maybe not a rock at all.

We didn't know. We didn't care. We had enough samples to show the kids what the eggs were all about and I didn't think anything more of it.

Another regret.

I let Quinn take the egg out of the glass. He dried it off and took it to the basement where he keeps his rocks and geodes. I figured he'd take a hammer to it and see what it was made of.

In hindsight, that was a bad decision.

But you don't know what you don't know.

This afternoon, the kids did their last dab of homework for the week, we had an early dinner, watched some TV then they went off to the basement to play while I stayed upstairs cleaning up the meal-time mess.

I wiped down the countertops in the kitchen. Cleaned up the dishes, started the dishwasher. Took the rag out to the dining room table and wiped it down. I smiled as I remembered Josey's shriek of joy at the first little triceratops that tumbled from the broken shell. I remember remembering because as I was thinking about Monday evening's display work, I heard another shrill, piercing shriek.

Coming from the basement.

But this one wasn't happy little girl delight. It carried a tone of anguish and fear. And pain. Like the time Quinn had built a ladder from the neighbor's leftover remodeling scraps and had Josey test it out. She'd made it to the top when the last rung split in two. I'd come out of the house just in time to see her fall from the ladder and hear the shriek as she toppled to the ground and broke her collar bone.

Same shriek now.

Before I could take two steps away from the table, I heard Quinn's slightly deeper moan followed by another shriek.

When I reached the basement steps, the kids were already halfway up.

Followed by that *thing*.

And orange flames grabbing for their feet from between the wooden steps.

———

MY COMPOSURE IS GONE NOW. REMEMBERING THE FIRE AND the creature. Remembering barely enough time to grab my keys and phone from the entryway table and escape out the front door.

The detective hands me a napkin. It smells of banana and peanut butter, but I wipe my face with it anyway.

"Quinn had burns on his calves. I want to see my children."

"Ma'am, the kids are well cared for. Right here in this building. We're getting their stories, too. Quinn's burns have been treated. He's doing well, I'm told." He touched the earpiece.

"I didn't think you could talk to minors without a parent present. I really do want that phone call now. I've cooperated. I want to see my children."

The detective stands and stretches. Again, his jacket opens and I see his service weapon. "Tell me about the creature. And then we'll tell you what we know."

"Who's we? I just called you a few hours ago. How could you know anything yet, when all you've got is my story?"

He flinches. Slightly, but he flinches. "Please, ma'am. Tell me about the creature."

I huff in frustration. Wanting this to be over, but not wanting to remember. Not wanting to see that expression on his face that every other first responder had given me. "Small, but not small. There's no way he came out of that egg and grew that fast. Thin, but not thin. Wings that spread out like a bat's only shimmering, like electric currents danced from his body and out over the tips. And its eyes—"

I pause to look at the man's face for signs of disbelief, but that's not the look he gave me. When I explained to the firemen and the EMTs what the kids and I saw, they looked at us with uncertainty. Curiosity. Some raised one eyebrow and nodded slowly. I must be crazy and I'd enlisted my poor kids to play along.

To create a most fantastical cover story as to why my house stood as nothing but a see-through ember shell and why my son's legs were burned.

This man. This man had understanding in his eyes. Knowing.

"Did you see the creature after the fire?"

"I was focused on my kids. I hoped the thing burned."

"It didn't. They don't burn."

Now my eyebrow goes up on one side and I nod my head in disbelief. He's mocking me. He looks up at the camera and nods. His best buddy comes through the windowless door again with a file folder and slides it across the table to me.

"Open it," he says. I don't comply. It was Friday when my house burnt to the ground. Maybe it's still Friday. Or Saturday now. I don't know. I won't comply until I get answers.

"We were the ones trying to contact you. We've been keeping an eye on shipments of this sort from that factory."

"Again, who's *we*?"

He takes his identification from his back pocket. In hindsight, I should've asked to see this tiny folded leather pouch when he first entered the room. But so many had entered and left. So many promises that my kids are fine and that if I tell this tale one more time, I'll see them soon.

I stare at the hefty gold and blue badge, and his headshot stares back at me with the same piercing green eyes. I slowly process what I'm seeing. He's speaking, but I'm only catching bits of it. He's not a detective. He's only wearing a Fishers uniform in a feeble attempt to make me more comfortable. I run my fingers over the letters on the badge. NSA.

"—were trying to contact you without raising alarm. You and your children are some of the luckier ones we've questioned. Actually, you're the only ones who've survived to give any kind of detail about the creature."

I stare at him, dumbfounded.

"Open it."

I take the corner of the manila file in my fingertips, as if I'll burn myself when I touch it, and I fling the folder open. I fan out the contents.

Photos of burned homes. A business in ashes, its sign, in Chinese characters, hangs in charcoaled defeat from above a busted glass door.

All with bright red "CONFIDENTIAL" stamped across the tops.

My heart thumps inside my ears as the last page, a sketch of the creature, startles me.

"We don't have photos of it. Is that accurate? Do you have any detail we could add to make it more complete?"

I find my voice. "The eyes are wrong."

"How so?"

"They dripped."

"Dripped?"

I hesitate.

"Look, Mrs. Callahan, there's nothing we won't believe at this point. We believe your story. We believe your children's versions. You've nothing to worry about from us. We just need your description."

"They dripped...lava."

He sat back in his seat and put his head in his hands. The first sign of humanness from him since he started my interview. He waved at the camera.

I waited for the door to open as quickly as it had before, but it remained closed.

"A rogue terrorist faction engineered this biological, uh, well, *weapon*. Smuggled it into toys and novelty items delivered to gas stations and junk shops. And school fundraiser groups." He sits back in his chair and unbuttons the top button of his shirt. "We think they're testing it. Seeing what these creatures can do. How much destruction they'll cause. If they can be contained."

"Where is it?"

"We don't know."

"How many are there?"

"A dozen. Maybe more. Maybe less."

"You don't know."

"No."

"Now what?" I can only think of my kids. We're homeless. Possessionless.

"Ma'am, we're going to ask that you and your children remain in our protective custody until we can decide what to do. Leaking this would be disastrous."

"Not warning people would be disastrous. There are more eggs —" I think of all the kids at the carnival. Tomorrow. Or is it today?

"We've already confiscated those. Sent someone as soon as you relayed that information to us. No worries there."

The door finally opens and my children, my two beautiful, terrified children fling themselves into my arms, and we all cry. I look down at Quinn's leg. It's wrapped in clean, white bandages. Josey's hair's a mess and she has chocolate smeared on her upper lip.

"No one's going to believe me, Mom," Quinn whispered. "About what happened. I didn't mean to let it out. I thought it was a geode. I didn't—" He sobs into my chest. I hold them both closer and sob with them.

He's feeling the heavy weight of hindsight.

"Not your fault, son. Not your fault." The agent pats him on the shoulder. "We'll see about making lodging arrangements for you." He scoops up the folder and returns my keys to me.

"What about my phone?"

"We can't risk this getting out and causing a panic, ma'am. I'm sorry. But one number has called over and over."

"Who?"

"A Sally Buchanan."

I moan.

"You're late for the carnival."

THE REMOVAL OF BLUE SKY

Light-years away, Programmers void of emotion design our present-day experiences to preserve the human race. But resources are limited, and when a little girl creates a connection transcending the protocols, something must be done to protect the system and the dark skies threatening to take over the world.

First seen in the anthology Future Visions Volume 3 edited by Brian J. Walton, "The Removal of Blue Sky" was B. A. Paul's first short story sale and also received L. Ron Hubbard's Writers of the Future honorable mention.

On my Promotion Day, I was thrilled to find I had been assigned a seven-year-old little girl, but I dared not show it. When they handed me her file, I simply nodded and followed along in the line of other flat-faced Promotion Day participants. She lived in Connecticut with her father, mother and two-year-old brother. Her previous Programmer was retired, and I was chosen to spend my days designing hers. And why the humans enjoyed the four-legged things, I'll never understand.

A slender technology specialist opened the steel door and nodded toward the room. "Here is where you'll review Samantha's years so far, sir. Buzz me when you've finished and I'll show you to the Machine Room." The emotionless lady left me to the child's file and video report.

My heart soared. I took a seat at the table and the orange holographic frame buzzed to life in front of me. I watched Samantha's conception, birth, first year celebration and on and on. I watched her scrape her knees and wake up with nightmares. I didn't like those parts, but her Programmer did right to allow them. She wouldn't learn and grow properly without some conflict and pain.

We aren't supposed to get attached to our assigned subjects. For the most part, we don't have feelings, not in the human sense, as most of those bits of our DNA were burned out a millennium ago for the sake of galactic peace, but once in a while, a tidbit of code must sneak through. I'm not sure I can remain distant from this precious child. We don't have children here.

We are grown, cultivated, and trained.

We are not born. We don't even have names.

We are what we do.

The video continued to play on through her first day of school and the loss of her front teeth. Human anatomy was the hardest subject during training. Everything had to be just right or you could damage the program and, thus, damage the human. One could err in engineering, and the human finds another house. One could err with the weather, and it rains too much or not enough. But usually, human anatomy is what hangs us up.

After an hour, I had watched nearly every second of Samantha Strewing's life in Connecticut. I committed every detail to memory to use in her mosaic later if needed.

But there, just at the end of the video, was a white Scottish Terrier, romping and frolicking with Sam in her backyard. There was no mention of a pet in her permanent records. Perhaps a neighbor's dog, or a visiting relative's program blended with hers for a moment.

I rang the buzzer and the same dull-eyed woman escorted me from the Viewing Room to the Machine Room.

"You'll return to the Viewing Room as needed to check on your human's progress." I nodded in understanding.

"She has a dog now. I didn't see any previous record of that."

The assistant shrugged. "Must be some mistake in the typed profile, because what you see on the screen is her reality."

She used the security disc embedded into her arm to open the steel door to the Machine Room. I gasped and she glared at me. Hundreds of millions of stations encircled the Machine. My classmates told me I was an error because I responded to everything with gasps or enthusiasm, but the sight was too much to behold. The holographs truly didn't do it justice.

The assistant showed me to my station. On either side of me sat other Programmers, snapping tiles into trays and stacking them for the Loaders to fit into the Machine.

I spent the first two days learning how to load Sam's trays with dreams to echo the day before; daily goings-on and unexpected twists that each twenty-four-hour cycle takes in a human's life. Luckily, Samantha's previous Programmer had several days already loaded in the Machine, so I had time to learn the rhythm of the system.

In eight Earth hours, we could load thirty days of a human's existence. The gridded tray was simple in design. Each one contained three hundred spots for different colored tiles. Management sent down the mosaic pieces, brightly colored tiles in every color imaginable, through a large tubing system that started in the ceiling of the room's dome and snaked out to white, velvet-lined boxes on each of our tables.

After the first shift, I was in love with the sound of the glass pieces whisking through the tubing and falling into the box on my table. But I kept that to myself as the other Programmers seemed not to even notice when the tubes would come to life all around us.

It was a Programmer's job to assemble the pieces into the trays, load them into the Machine, then remove the trays once the day was spent. We dumped the tiles into the recycle bin to be cleaned and polished, and Management would send us a new batch.

By day four, Samantha was living in the world I created for her. She had free will, of course, but the systems in her life, her environment, and her body, those were controlled by us. By me. And the little dog was a permanent fixture now. I sent a note to Management so they could update her typed file.

On day five, I visited the Viewing Room to play back Sam's days since I took over. Her smile made me smile, and I ducked my head so the video camera in the corner of the room wouldn't catch me enjoying her life. She loved to play outside, so I made sure the first few days I gave her were filled with sun and blue sky so she and the Scotty could enjoy each other's company.

The tiles that created weather combinations were the most glorious of them all. Bright azure, cobalt and indigo swirled with the tiniest bits of white for wispy clouds and gentle breezes. Citrine and amber streaked with crimson and rose for glorious sunrises, and bright yellow for midday. I had to be careful in the Machine Room, too, or my counterparts would surely spot the enjoyment I had sorting through the colors in the white box.

On day twenty-eight, the tubes sparked to life, and the whisk of the tiles sliding in a million directions filled the room. I sat up a little straighter in anticipation. The new batch slid into the velvet with soft clinks and I dumped some of the tiles onto my table. I thumbed through them, looking for the blues and yellows, but only found yellows and grays. I dumped the rest of them, as well, but I did not see the first blue tile. Not even a shade remotely close to blue. I only had three more trays to fill for the shift, and I was forced to give Samantha a rainy weekend, but she wouldn't experience it for over a month.

I glanced toward the other Programmers' stations and didn't see any blue on their tables, either. But none of them seemed concerned. Their hands blurred as they snapped tile after tile into place for their assigned humans.

At the end of the shift, I found an Assistant outside the doors of the Viewing Room. "Would you like me to set up a video file for you, sir?" she asked.

"No. Not today. I have another question, though."

She nodded.

"Where are all the blue tiles? Not one blue tile was sent to my box today."

She stared at me with her blank face. "Management is cutting back on blue tiles."

"Why?" I tried to keep mine blank as well.

"The raw materials are running low, and it's cost prohibitive to find another source at this time."

Her answer sounded rehearsed, though there wasn't a line of Programmers asking about the missing blue tiles.

"I thought we recycled everything. I thought there would be enough for forever."

"The blues degrade more quickly than the others, and since they're chosen more often than any other color, we've run very low."

"So no human will have blue skies?"

"We're working on a solution."

"Do you understand what this means to them?"

Her blank face broke into a glare. I'd gone too far. She raised her arm to her mouth and called Management.

"I have a Programmer who's showing raw emotion. Please

advise." She tilted her head, and I heard a muffled reply through her earpiece.

"You are to wait here with me until Management comes."

I turn to leave, but Management was already on the Viewing Room floor. Two members escorted me to the end of the hallway and through double granite doors into a waiting area. They glared down at me. My heart beat its way into my feet and sweat started across my forehead. That doesn't happen very often, either. The sweats are a dead giveaway that one is overly emotional.

A second set of doors opened and a gray-haired lady motioned for me to join her. I walked into her office and sat across from her.

"The Assistant told me what happened. Why did you react so strongly?"

I choked back the lump in my throat. "I think removing blue sky from Earth is a mistake."

"We are working on a solution. We have thirty Earth days to solve the problem. That's lots of time for us." The lady's face was blank, but her eyes were kind. And they were the same color of blue as Samantha's favorite sky.

"Don't we have any blue tiles left? Any at all?" Without permission, and certainly without intention, a single tear escaped my right eye and ran down my cheek.

The elder watched with an expressionless face as I reached up to dry it away.

"I think it's time we retire you, Programmer." There was no malice in her voice. I felt a wave of peace and mercy wash over the room. "I assure you, we'll find a solution. But this show of emotion is dangerous to our existence."

"What will I do? I'm a Programmer. I only just started."

"I think you and your predecessor will work well together for the rest of your days." She pressed a button on the edge of her desk and the Management men escorted me out of the elder's office.

Confusion and grief marked the first several days in my new position. The barred and barren environment, and the form I had taken, was so disorienting that I cried out loud most of the time.

Then I saw her. Right in front of me stood the little girl that stole my heart and made me smile real smiles. My whole body trembled in anticipation. I couldn't stop shaking.

She picked me up and wrapped her small arms around me.

"This one. I want this one, Daddy. Scout will love him!" Samantha kissed my head and slung me over her shoulder.

We stepped outside and everything was gray. And white. And black. There was no color to anything.

Then I remembered my training. Canines only saw in shades of gray.

Sam took me to her home. To her back yard. And to the Scotty that I watched her play with and love for hours on end in the Viewing Room. And the Scotty was like me. We knew each other, even though communication was strange and difficult. He was my predecessor.

I sat in the grass and watched her play with Scout, not sure what to do. Samantha motioned for me to join them.

She called me Sunny.

She gave me a name.

Above, the heavy grays and dark smokiness began to brighten. A white glowing globe lit up the yard and warmed my back.

"Mommy! Mommy! Look! It's blue again! I can see the blue sky again!"

I barked. Scout barked back. We played and chased all afternoon.

I couldn't see the colors anymore, but I knew she could.

And that's all that matters.

Beth enjoys chucking words into sentences then standing back to see what magic—or mayhem—falls out, crafting tales in mystery, sci-fi, fantasy, and general "slice of life" fiction. She couldn't accomplish this without the help of her tutu-clad Little Miss Muse and Trudi the Concrete Office Goose, who's partial to superhero capes.

Her stories have appeared in multiple publications, including Pulphouse Fiction Magazine and Ellery Queen Mystery Magazine, and in multiple fiction anthologies. She's received several Honorable Mentions from Writers of the Future. Her lighthearted blog peeks into the writing life as she pokes fun at herself and her circus of a life.

Follow the antics of Little Miss Muse and Trudi, read Beth's blog (she might have burned down her kitchen last week), and discover the stories at bapaul.com.

Short Story Collections

Spunk and Spice, Volumes 1 and 2: A Collection of six short stories celebrating timeless wit and wisdom.

Out There, Volumes 1 and 2: A Collection of six short sci-fi and speculative tales.

Mystery Minutes, Volumes 1 and 2: Six short mystery stories

All the Feels, Volumes 1, 2, and 3: Collections of inspiring short stories

Just a Tick of Whimsy, Volumes 1 and 2: Collections of fantasy shorts.

Hijacked Holidays: Definitely not your warm-and-fuzzy winter tales.

Dark Minds: Toe-curling twisted mysteries.

Blog Compilations: Slices of the writing life with lots of laughs and bumps in the road.

Life Along the Way

Life All Over Again

Novels

Triage

Young Adult (or Young at Heart) Books

Switch: Book 1 in the Oliver Andrews Trilogy

STAY IN TOUCH!

BAPAUL.COM

Take a glimpse into B.A. Paul's writing journey, including the ups and downs of managing family, "real jobs," ducks in wobbling rows, and chasing down her Little Miss Muse. New blog posts go up Mondays, with the first Monday of the month reserved for a free fiction short story available on the blog for a limited time.

Newsletter Signup!

Get the latest release information, author updates, and exclusive content by signing up at bapaul.com.